The Jellybean Society

a cartoon collection by
Pat Oliphant

Foreword by Larry L. King

Andrews and McMeel, Inc.
A Universal Press Syndicate Company
Kansas City • New York • Washington

ISBN: 0-8362-1250-9
Library of Congress Catalog Card Number: 81-68676

For Mary Ann

Foreword

Pat Oliphant is my favorite curmudgeon.

Mr. Webster defines "curmudgeon" as follows: "A gruff or irritable person, especially an elderly man."

I see no reason to quibble with Mr. Webster.

Two or three times weekly I break bread with Old Man Oliphant, usually at a fake English pub on Capitol Hill, where he refuses to eat meat or sit near children. Should either come near him he froths and foams.

Oliphant is habitually late, probably because he has been rehearsing his laments and diatribes against the world's latest frauds and outrages. Before he has properly settled onto his bar stool he begins to bark challenges and invectives. Just when it appears he is certain to graduate from curmudgeony to apoplexy, Oliphant breaks into huge guffaws. Presumably, these laughing fits celebrate the world's insanities and his left-handed appreciation of them.

A good cartoonist—and I must admit I believe Pat Oliphant to be the best—probably needs to agitate himself to make certain his quill will emit the correct measures of acids, salts, and poisons.

Should a cartoonist go around all smiles and handshakes while urging his associates to "Have a good day," he likely would lose his membership card in the Amalgamated Brotherhood of Character Assassins, Stuffed Shirt Pluckers, and Balloon Prickers. Also, he would draw some mighty dull cartoons.

While Oliphant is a man of many strong dislikes, he also has his preferences. The best I can figure he likes the fruit of the grape, W.C. Fields, vegetables, cheese-and-onion sandwiches, the West and Southwest, brunettes of busty architecture, drawing dirty pictures he refuses to sign, and watching folks slip on banana peels. Nobody's perfect.

Insult one of Oliphant's likes and he may stab you with his pen. When numerous erring congressmen—caught in the Abscam net or in sexual transgressions—were quick to publicly blame their troubles on whiskey, Pat Oliphant sprang to the drawing board. He concocted a drink-sipping statesman—in bed with two floozies and a cowboy—who, while receiving a parade of Arabs bearing bundles of boodle, is made to say: "Dear me, all this booze is making me do things I wouldn't normally do as a congressman."

As one who believes that twentieth-century man and his predecessors have mindlessly violated Mother Nature, Oliphant is hard on public figures who ignore ecological considerations. When Ronald Reagan made a thoughtless remark slighting trees, he showed up in Oliphant's panel looking unusually prune-faced. Reagan's secretary of interior, James Watt — whom Oliphant suspects of hating mountains and of wanting to dynamite fish—may be found in the company of pussel-gutted oil tycoons and himself looks like a cut-rate undertaker. Cartooning is not for the timid.

One who follows Oliphant consistently will be able to judge his state of mind about a given public figure over the long haul. I fancy I can tell when President Reagan has done something that pleases Oliphant: There are not so many age lines in his face. Jimmy Carter began in Oliphant's panels as a normal, regular-sized fellow when he came fresh to Washington. He became smaller and smaller, much like the Incredible Shrinking Man, so that soon his feet failed to touch the floor when he sat. By the time of the 1980 presidential campaign, the Georgian was reduced to a baby's high chair in the Oliphant view. Turns out the voters felt pretty much the same way.

When the U.S. government is guilty of some particularly odious folly, Oliphant draws Uncle Sam as a boozy, blundering W.C. Fields. This causes the cartoonist to get some pretty irate mail questioning his patriotism. I find this ironic, knowing how secretly proud the old curmudgeon is of the U.S. citizenship he chose a few years ago.

This son-of-Australia finds it strange that no matter how foolish or venal he draws public figures, a high percentage beg him for the original cartoon and then request that he sign it for them. Considering this a perversion against normal conduct, he usually refuses.

Now and then Oliphant enjoys playing tricks on his subjects. Spotting some senator, congressman, or diplomat in a restaurant, he may draw their likeness on a napkin and have it delivered surreptitiously to their tables. Since Oliphant rarely permits his picture to be published and largely eschews TV appearances, not everyone can easily spot him. He enjoys sitting innocently while the Big Shots look around the room in hopes of discovering him, and is particularly delighted when they accuse some bewildered stranger of being Pat Oliphant. On occasion, he has firmly denied that he is Pat Oliphant himself.

Yes, Old Man Oliphant **is** something of a weird eccentric—but, then, had he been a normal boy he probably would not have grown up to be a cartoonist. It is difficult to imagine Pat Oliphant in any other role — he having won every major award that can be bestowed upon a member of his peculiar art and sullen craft, including the coveted Pulitzer. Why, Dartmouth University even hauled off and made him a Doctor of Letters this year! Dr. Oliphant finds this accolade as amusing as I do, except when I beg him for prescriptions. ("Doctor, I'll have a handful of greenies and some red 'uns and how about throwin' in a few of them black beauties?")

I'm glad that Dr. Oliphant does what he does for a living. It keeps him off the streets and the welfare roles without causing him to stoop to honest work. And, meanwhile, he provides the rest of us with grand entertainment—not to mention food for thought.

May the old curmudgeon keep on curmudgeoning.

—Larry L. King,
(Who is co-author,
The Best Little Whorehouse in Texas,
has no national radio show, and is
not married to Billy Jean.)

'MOST AIR POLLUTION IS CAUSED BY TREES... NOW TO GO AFTER ALL THOSE BUMS ON UNEMPLOYMENT INSURANCE!'

August 21, 1980

LISTENING FOR THE TANKS

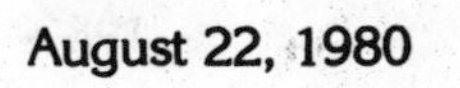
August 22, 1980

August 29, 1980

'DESIST, WOMAN! WERE YOU NOT ONCE A HOMELESS WAIF, YOURSELF?'

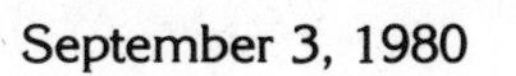

September 3, 1980

September 5, 1980

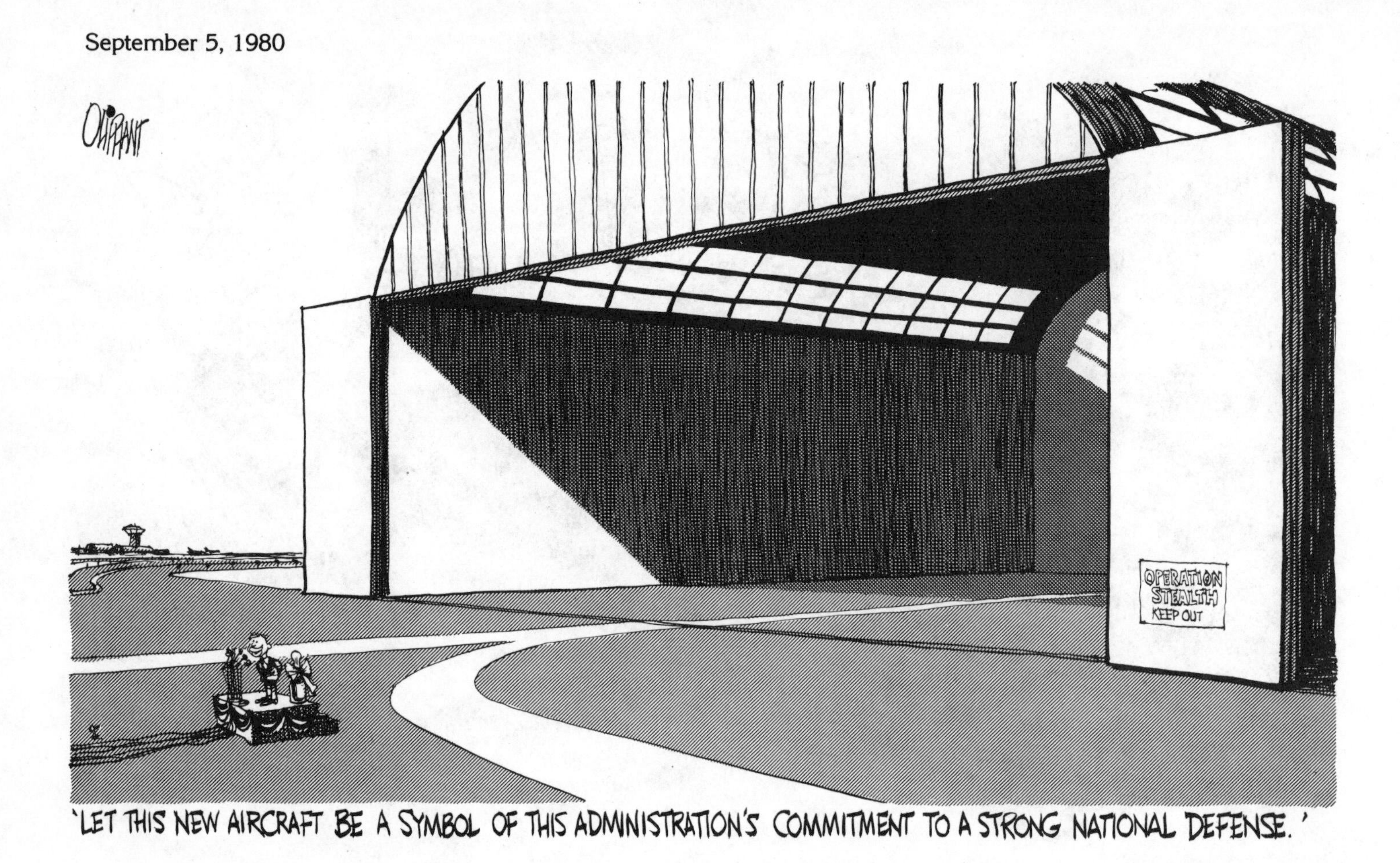

'LET THIS NEW AIRCRAFT BE A SYMBOL OF THIS ADMINISTRATION'S COMMITMENT TO A STRONG NATIONAL DEFENSE.'

September 8, 1980

'THINK—THINK HARD! ABBIE HOFFMAN, THE FAMOUS YIPPIE... UP AGAINST THE WALL! DON'T TRUST ANYONE OVER THIRTY! OFF THE PIGS! THE CHICAGO SEVEN! TRY TO REMEMBER...'

September 9, 1980

'... THEN, IN ADDITION TO THE ANNUAL AND MONTHLY DUES, THERE'LL BE YOUR ORGANIZING DUES, YOUR ASSESSMENTS FOR THE STRIKE FUND, THE MEDICAL AND HOSPITALIZATION FUND, UNION OFFICERS' SALARIES, GENERAL OPERATING EXPENSES, THE ANNUAL PICNIC...'

September 11, 1980

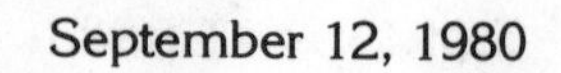

September 12, 1980

'I'M SORRY, GENTLEMEN — IT'S NOT EASY FOR US JEWISH VOTERS TO DECIDE WHICH UNSMART, BORN-AGAIN, FUNDAMENTALIST GENTILE WE WANT FOR PRESIDENT.'

September 15, 1980

September 19, 1980

September 24, 1980

September 26, 1980

September 29, 1980

'... THEN MR. CARTER SAID OK WITH REAGAN BUT NOT WITH ANDERSON. THEN MR. REAGAN SAID ALL THREE OR NOTHING. THEN WE HAD ANOTHER DEBATE PROPOSAL, BUT FLORENCE HERE FORGOT TO MAIL OUT THE INVITATIONS.'

September 30, 1980

'BEGGING THE ADMIRAL'S PARDON, BUT ALL HANDS ARE ON DECK, SIR.'

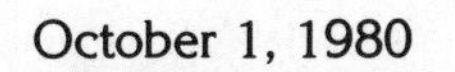

October 1, 1980

'WHY, JIMMY, SURE I'LL VOTE TO KEEP CARTER IN THE WHITE HOUSE — BUT, HAIL, DO YOU RECKON Y'ALL CAN RUN THE GAS STATION?'

October 3, 1980

October 6, 1980

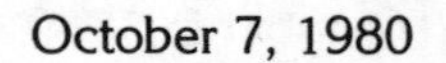

October 7, 1980

"...AND NOW, IF YOU'LL TURN TO PAGE 27 OF MY NEWEST BOOK OF INSPIRATIONAL HYMNS (YOURS FREE WITH A FIFTY DOLLAR CONTRIBUTION), LET US SING TOGETHER, "IF HE'S GOOD ENOUGH FOR JESUS, HE'S GOOD ENOUGH FOR ME"."

GREAT ISSUES OF 1980

October 10, 1980

'DEAR ME, ALL THIS BOOZING IS MAKING ME DO THINGS I WOULDN'T NORMALLY DO AS A CONGRESSMAN.'

October 13, 1980

'WHEN YOU CAN'T SEE THE TREES FOR THE SMOG, THEN I SAY IT'S TIME TO GET RID OF THE DAM' TREES!'

October 14, 1980

October 15, 1980

'AND NOW I GIVE YOU THE MAN WHO GAVE US THE REFUGEES, AND RIGHT NOW IS TURNING LOOSE OUR PRISONERS IN CUBA, A FRIEND IN NEED, A GREAT GUY AND A BEAUTIFUL HUMAN BEING, LET'S HEAR IT FOR...'

October 17, 1980

'HOW WOULD YOU LIKE TO BE ON THE SUPREME COURT?'

October 20, 1980

A HORSE RACE... THE VOTERS' POINT OF VIEW

October 22, 1980

'THE REGULAR GUYS FEEL YOU'RE GOING TO SCREW UP THE TAX-EXEMPT DEAL FOR ALL OF US.'

'WELL, I'VE DECIDED!.. I'VE DECIDED VOTING ONLY ENCOURAGES THEM.'

October 30, 1980

'LEE IACOCCA SENT US!'

November 3, 1980

November 4, 1980

November 5, 1980

LANDSLIDE

November 6, 1980

'WELCOME BACK, CONGRESSMAN.'

November 12, 1980

MUSIC OF THE PLANETS

November 14, 1980

MR. CARTER RETURNS TO LOW-PROFILE TRANQUILITY IN PLAINS

November 17, 1980

Dear Uncle Sugar
Nothing is working
here in Poland.

POLISH
PEOPLES
REPUBLIC

The country is broke, we're
up to our ears in debt
and there's no way we
can pay our
bills.

GLORIOUS
POLISH
PEOPLES
REPUBLIC

Why, our new workers' union won't
even recognize the supremacy of
the Communist System!

INVINCIBLE
REPUBLIC
OF POLAND

Please lend us
$3 billion at once.

IN SMALL,
UNMARKED
BILLS
OF COURSE
!

OLIPHANT

November 18, 1980

'THE COWBOY IS COMING! THE COWBOY IS COMING!'

November 21, 1980

CONGRESSIONAL STROKIN' TIME

November 24, 1980

'FORGIVE ME, ALGERNON, BUT I REALLY MUST BE RUNNING ALONG. THERE'S A GENTLEMAN HERE TO SEE ME FROM THE FEDERAL BUREAU OF EXCESSIVE SPORTS VIOLENCE.'

'HERE... YOU MAY NEED THIS.'

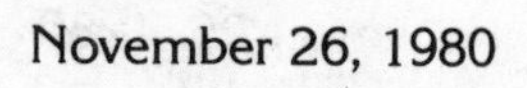

November 26, 1980

'SEE? IT'S QUITE SAFE, AND VERY THERAPEUTIC!'

November 28, 1980

KING OF THE HILL

December 1, 1980

December 2, 1980

'THE BAD NEWS IS, I'M BROKE THIS YEAR. THE GOOD NEWS IS, I'M EXPECTING TO BE OFFERED A CABINET POSITION.'

December 3, 1980

'WE DARE NOT SEND OUR SOVIET HORDES IN THERE — THAT DEVIL, WASELA, WILL ORGANIZE THEM!'

December 9, 1980

December 10, 1980

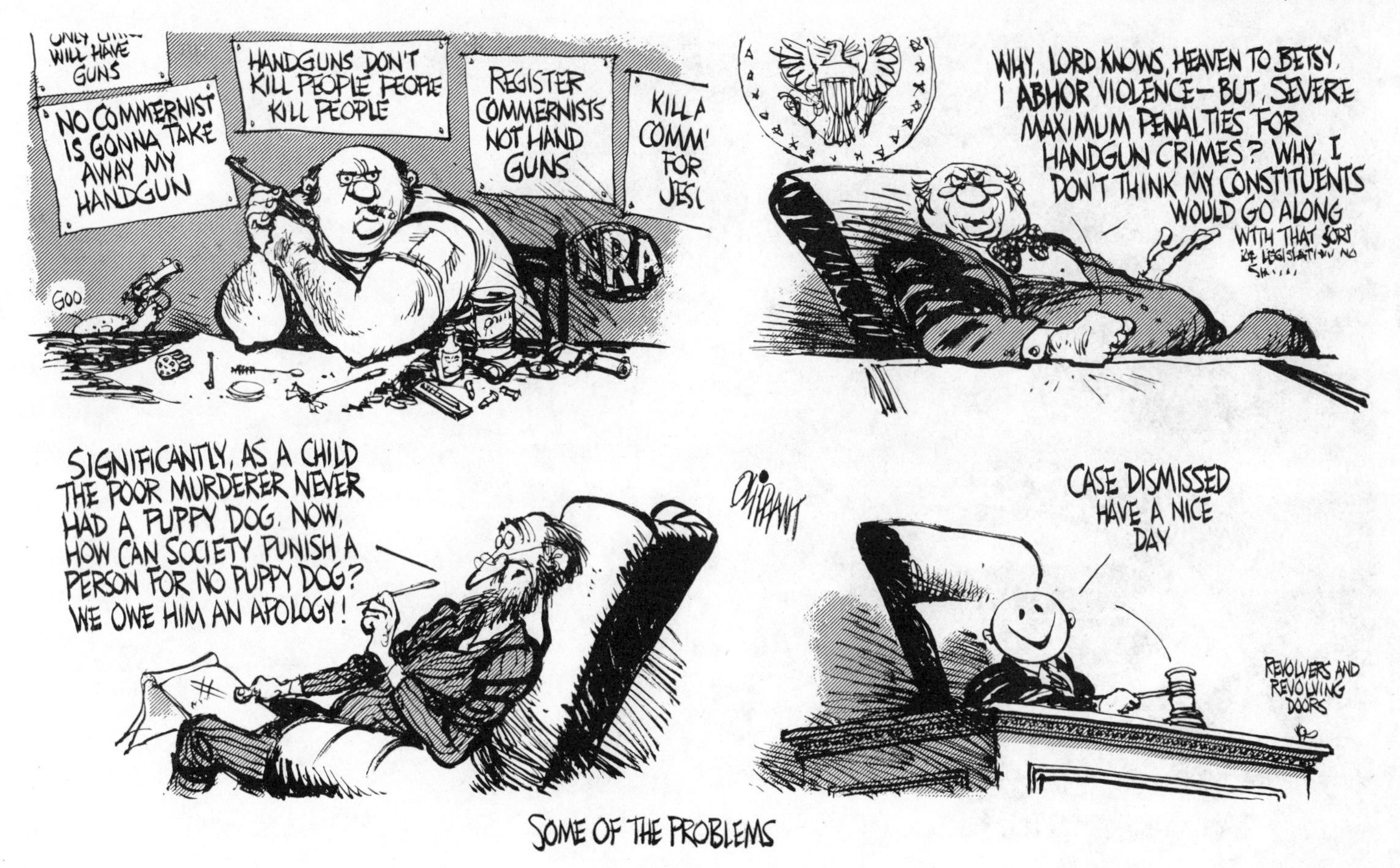

SOME OF THE PROBLEMS

December 12, 1980

'AND YET, A LITTLE BIRD KEPT TELLING ME, "AL HAIG FOR STATE, AL HAIG FOR STATE"...'

'WELL, SO FAR, SO GOOD...'

December 16, 1980

'MRS. REAGAN SEEMS TO BE HINTING AT SOMETHING, ROSALYNN...'

December 17, 1980

'HOLD STEADY, MEN — OUR SHOW OF UNITY SEEMS TO HAVE THEM BAMBOOZLED.'

December 18, 1980

AL HAIG, THE BAGGAGE CARRIER.

December 19, 1980

'MAY I SPEAK TO DAVE WINFIELD, PLEASE?... YES, IT IS RATHER URGENT.'

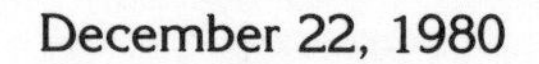
December 22, 1980

December 24, 1980

'YOU, MADAM, ARE THE RAPEE-DESIGNATE — I'LL JUST BE HERE TO SEE IT'S ALL LEGAL.'

December 26, 1980

'GOLLY! YOU SOREHEADS HAVE TO BLAME US DEMOCRATS FOR EVERY LITTLE THING!'

December 31, 1980

'BLAST! THERE'S ANOTHER ONE!'

January 5, 1981

'WELL, WHATEVER IT IS, IT JUST HAS TO BE BETTER THAN THE AWFUL SLOP IN THE LAST FOUR BOTTLES.'

OF HUMAN RITES

January 8, 1981

January 9, 1981

'SAY, WHO WAS THAT MASKED MAN? ... AND WHAT THE HELL IS HE DOING HERE WITHOUT PORTFOLIO..?'

January 12, 1981

'DON'T RUSH ME — FIRST, I HAVE TO FIND THE HEAD END.'

January 13, 1981

January 14, 1981

'NO, MAN, THIS AIN'T THE WAY TO NO 'NAUGURAL BALL — THIS HERE DUNKIRK!'

January 15, 1981

'RIGHT NOW HE'S PROBABLY ASKING NANCY IF HE NEEDS TO PACK A SWEATER.'

January 16, 1981

'MESSAGE FROM HEADQUARTERS..."IF YOU KNOW A BETTER HOLE, GO TO IT".'

HE ENTERED THE OVAL OFFICE. THE CHAIR— HIS CHAIR! SAT EMPTY BEHIND THE PRESIDENT'S DESK— HIS DESK! 'WELL, GEE!' HE GULPED, 'THIS IS IT... THIS IS REALLY IT!!
BUT WHAT UNKNOWN DANGERS LURKED BEHIND THAT DESK??
'WELL, GOSH,' HE SAID GRIMLY, 'I'LL NEVER FIND OUT BY STANDING HERE!' THE PHONE RANG
JELLY BEANS
OLIPHANT
Mr. President
RONALD REAGAN
with
NANCY & introducing
ED MEESE
QUIET ON THE SET!

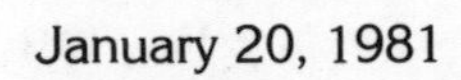

January 20, 1981

'YOUR SHIP, CAPTAIN!'

O, SAY, CAN YOU SEE...

January 21, 1981

January 22, 1981

'WHAT'S THIS? OH, THE OLD EXECUTIVE ORDER FOR A BREEDING FREEZE ... SAY, DID ANYONE EVER TELL YOU YOU'RE KINDA CUTE?'

January 23, 1981

'NOW ALL WE BARBARIANS HAVE IS EACH OTHER!'

January 27, 1981

'...AND HOW DOES IT FEEL TO BE A RETURNEE? AND WHAT IS IT LIKE TO BE ABLE TO TAKE A WALK ALONE? AND WHAT WAS THE FIRST THING YOU SAID TO YOUR RELATIVES? AND HOW DO YOU FEEL ABOUT IRAN? AND WHAT IS YOUR REACTION TO BEING HOME?'

January 28, 1981

'AS YOU MAY HAVE NOTICED, WE HAVE A PRESSING MUTUAL PROBLEM...'

January 29, 1981

'HOW WAS I?'

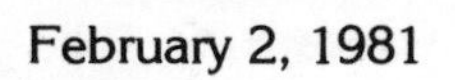
February 2, 1981

'WELL, I DON'T CARE WHAT REAGAN SAYS ... I STILL THINK YOU'RE CUTE AND CUDDLY.'

'WHERE WAS I WHEN THE PARADE PASSED BY..?'

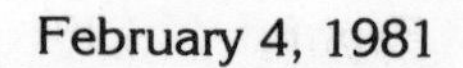

February 4, 1981

'YOU MAY BE ABLE TO PICK UP A COPY OF 'PENTHOUSE' AT THE NEXT NEWS STAND — IF YOU CAN GET THERE AHEAD OF THE REVEREND FALWELL.'

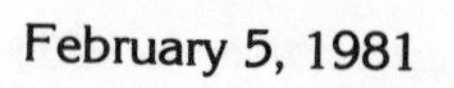

February 5, 1981

'HAW! THAT TICKLES!'

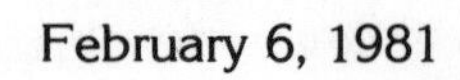

February 6, 1981

'ANY TIME YOU PUT THAT MANY CANDLES ON A BIRTHDAY CAKE, YOU GOT TROUBLE!'

February 10, 1981

THE STOCKMAN COMETH

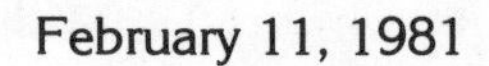

February 11, 1981

'YOU CAN'T DO THIS — I'M A LIBERAL! I DON'T AGREE WITH JUSTICE BURGER! I THINK WE SHOULD KEEP THE STREETS SAFE FOR CRIMINALS! I DON'T MIND IF YOU CLUTTER UP THE JUSTICE SYSTEM! WAIT...'

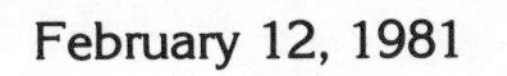
February 12, 1981

' "CANCEL SATURDAY DELIVERY"—HECK, JUST WHEN WE WUZ GAININ' ON IT!'

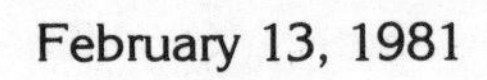
February 13, 1981

LANDING RUNNING

'I SUGGEST YOU START DRILLING HERE... IF WE DEFILE THE BOSS'S HOME STATE FIRST, IT WILL HELP WITH OUR—AH—PUBLIC CREDIBILITY, LATER.'

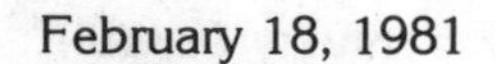

February 18, 1981

'OF COURSE IT'S A REAL BOMB—BUT IF WE TOLD RON THAT, IT WOULD RUIN HIS CONCENTRATION.'

February 20, 1981

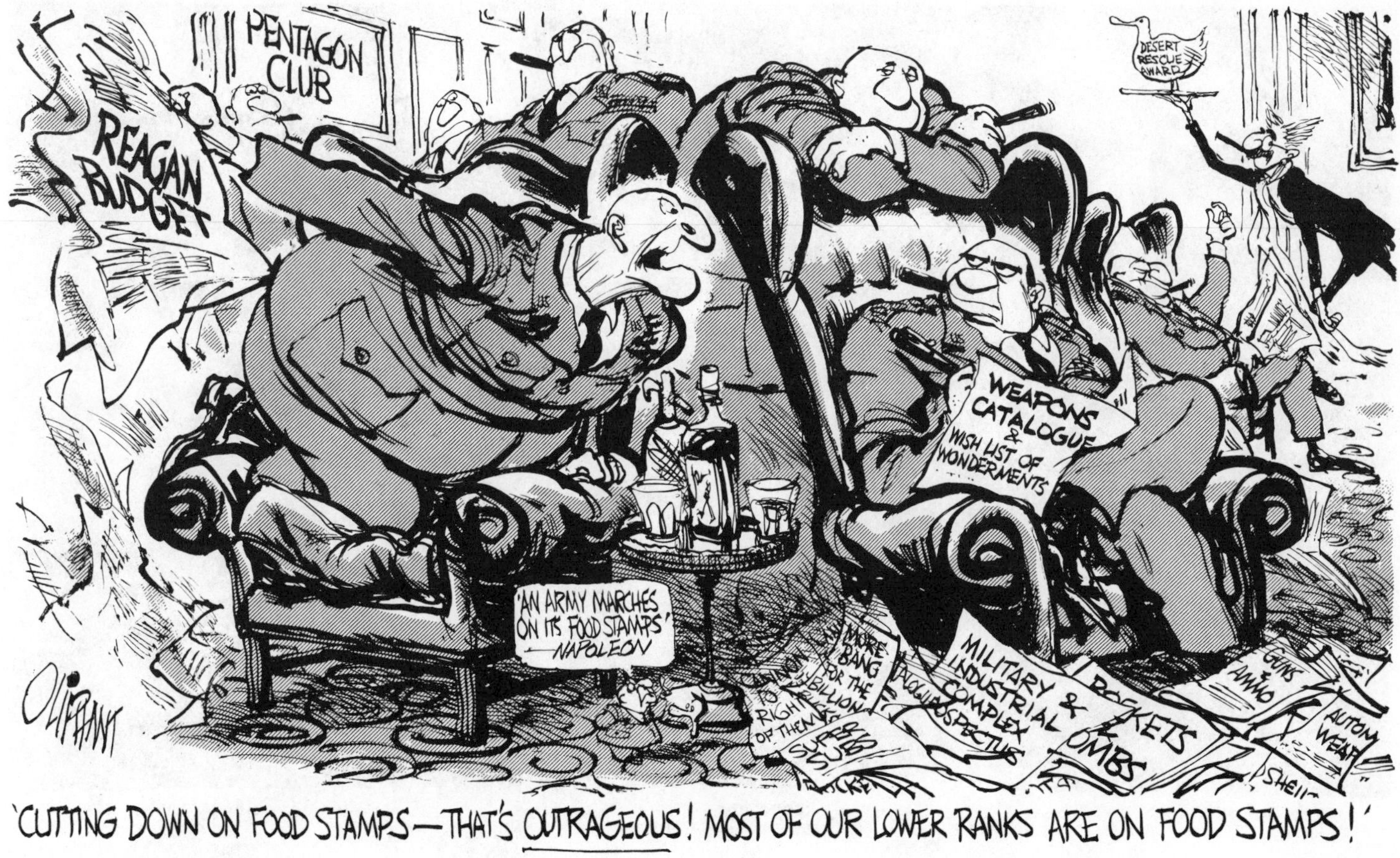

'CUTTING DOWN ON FOOD STAMPS—THAT'S OUTRAGEOUS! MOST OF OUR LOWER RANKS ARE ON FOOD STAMPS!'

February 23, 1981

SHUTTLEBUTT

February 24, 1981

'HOLD REAL STILL, SAM... I'LL JUST KNOCK THE ASH OFF HIS CIGAR.'

February 25, 1981

February 26, 1981

'I MUST SAY, SMEDLEY, THESE ANNOUNCEMENTS JUST AREN'T THE SAME SINCE RUPERT MURDOCH BOUGHT THE TIMES!'

February 27, 1981

'THERE'S BEEN A SLIGHT MISCALCULATION IN OUR BASE FIGURES, SO FOR THE PURPOSES OF THIS PRESENTATION WE MUST ASK YOU TO THINK IN BILLIONS INSTEAD OF MILLIONS.'

March 2, 1981

THE LIGHT AT THIS END OF THE TUNNEL

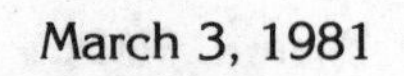
March 3, 1981

'A GROUP IN MICHIGAN HAS ORGANIZED A TAX REVOLT—ARREST MICHIGAN!'

March 4, 1981

'LOSE ONE THROW. RELINQUISH LUNCH MONEY. DO NOT PASS GO. PENTAGON TAKES FREE JUMP TO EL SALVADOR.'

March 5, 1981

OLIPHANT
DAIRY FARMERS
PRICE SUPPORTS
LUCKY US-
WE PAY
FOR IT
COMING
AND GOING!

'COULDN'T YOU AT LEAST TRY TO TRUST DAN RATHER?'

March 9, 1981

'WELL, MY ADVISER IS UNCLE SAM, AND UNCLE SAM SAYS...'

'PERSONALLY, I'M PEOPLE-ORIENTED,' CLAIMS THE INTERIOR SECRETARY.

March 11, 1981

'I SAY, WHAT JOLLY GOOD LUCK TO FIND YOU HERE, DEAR BOY — Y'KNOW, I DO BELIEVE THESE SILLY NINNIES ACTUALLY BWOUGHT ME OVER FWOM LONDON TO BWEED WITH THAT PERFECTLY DWEADFUL OLD BAT OVER THERE!'

March 12, 1981

'GORED OX, AGAIN.'

March 13, 1981

'HOW COME THE MEDICAL EXPERTS ARE ALWAYS THE LAST TO KNOW?'

'WELL, YES, STRICTLY SPEAKING THE CIA'S JOB IS ABROAD. HOWEVER, WE WERE NEVER VERY GOOD AT THE OVERSEAS SPYING, SO THEY'VE DECIDED WE SHOULD STICK TO THIS DOMESTIC STUFF.'

March 18, 1981

'OF COURSE, YOU'RE ALL WELCOME TO COME BACK ONCE THE COUNTRY'S TURNED ROUND.'

March 19, 1981

NO SAFETY NET

March 20, 1981

March 24, 1981

THE EIGHTEEN CENT ACT

March 25, 1981

'THIS IS HER BIGGEST IDEA SINCE SHE ENDORSED TEDDY FOR PRESIDENT.'

March 26, 1981

March 27, 1981

March 31, 1981

April 1, 1981

FIRST, THE PRESIDENT, THEN WHATSISNAME, AND THEN YOURS TRULY, ME!!
IN ROUGHLY THAT ORDER!
OLIPHANT

CRISIS MOVE #1: CLAP AL HAIG IN IRONS IMMEDIATELY.

SEALED CRISIS ORDERS
V.P.
EYES ONLY

April 2, 1981

'WE EUROPEANS, OF COURSE, HAVE NOTHING BUT CONTEMPT FOR YOUR AMERICAN PASSION FOR VIOLENCE—HOWEVER...'

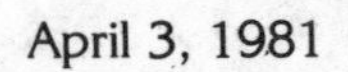
April 3, 1981

'A REPORTER FROM THE NATIONAL ENQUIRER, MISS BURNETT, WOULD LIKE A STATEMENT FROM YOU ON FUNDAMENTAL PRESS FREEDOMS.'

April 6, 1981

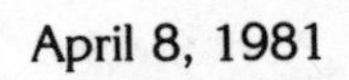

April 8, 1981

HEY, MICHELANGELO — YOU BETTER KNOCK IT OFF! THE POPE'S CUTTING OFF THE ARTS ENDOWMENT FUNDING!
OLIPHANT

April 10, 1981

'WELL, OLD DEAR, SEEING I'M HERE, AND SEEING YOUR OLD BOYFWEND IS BEING SUCH A SMASHING SPORT ABOUT ALL THIS, I EXPECT WE SHOULD MUDDLE ON THWOUGH... HELLO, DO I HAVE YOUR ATTENTION?'

April 24, 1981

April 28, 1981

'GOT THE IDEA? OK, NOW LET'S SEE YOU DO IT.'

April 30, 1981

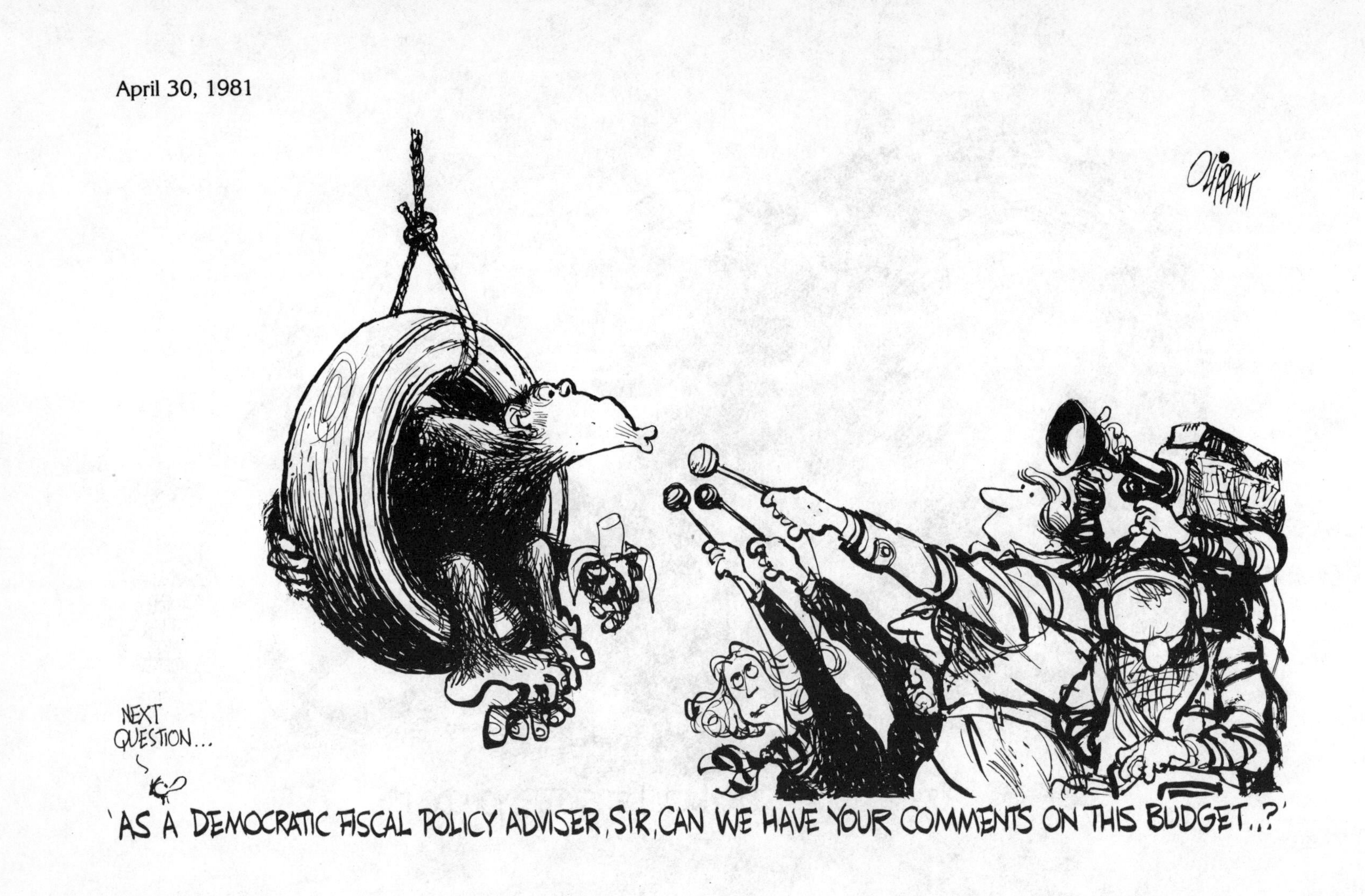

May 4, 1981

OLIPHANT

UAW

MADE IN DETROIT

WHERE ARE YOU, NADER SAN?

'THERE WAS A TIME WHEN ANYTHING MADE IN JAPAN WAS TRASHY JUNK — BUT I ALWAYS KNEW THAT, GIVEN THE CHANCE, WE COULD BEAT THEM AT THEIR OWN GAME.'

May 5, 1981

THE DEMOCRATIC ALTERNATIVE

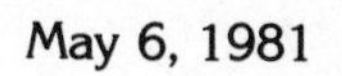

May 6, 1981

HOME TO ROOST

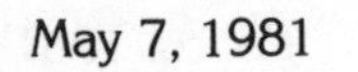
May 7, 1981

'WELL, IF WE CAN'T PUT IT OUT HERE, PERHAPS YOU HAVE SOME SUGGESTIONS WHERE WE COULD PUT IT...!'

May 8, 1981

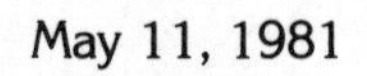
May 11, 1981

WHAT WE HAVE HERE IS THE STOCKMAN SPECIAL SENIOR CITIZEN SOCIAL SECURITY SAFETY® NET
HOW CAN WE IMPROVE THIS NET? OBSERVE...
OLIPHANT
SNIP
SNIP SNIP
SNIP
NOW WE HAVE A NET WITH EVEN FEWER HOLES THAN BEFORE!
NEW
IMPROVED

May 12, 1981

'JUST FLIP 'EM ON THEIR BACKS, ALEX —THEY CAN'T BE ANY TOUGHER THAN CONGRESSMEN.'

May 13, 1981

'BUT THE PRESIDENT HAS BEEN REAL NICE ABOUT IT. HE CUT THEIR SOCIAL SECURITY BENEFITS, BUT HE'S ENCOURAGING THEM TO WORK PAST 65... G'NIGHT GRAN'MA.'

May 15, 1981

'ANYBODY GOT ANY USE FOR A THIN, WIDE LIBERAL?'

May 15, 1981

TREED

May 19, 1981

JUST ONCE ROUND THE BLOCK FOR ELECTION TIME
THE PEACE CANDIDATE

May 20, 1981

May 21, 1981

...AND IF ANY OF THOSE ENVIRONMENTAL PESTS GIVE YOU ANY LIP, YOU JUST TELL 'EM WHO SENT YOU!!
OK, DAD
WATT
OH,OH...THE ENVIRONMENTALISTS VERSUS THE FUNDAMENTALISTS
OLIPHANT

May 22, 1981

'<u>AHA</u>!! HOLDING HANDS! THAT'S THE BEGINNING OF LIFE — NEXT THING WE KNOW SHE'LL WANT AN <u>ABORTION</u>!'

May 25, 1981

SENIOR CITIZENS'
WALLOP-THE-PRESIDENT DAY
BRING YOUR OWN STICK
ALOHA
WHY DON'T HE PICK ON FOLKS HIS OWN AGE?
OLIPHANT

May 28, 1981

'WHY DO I CADDY FOR YOU? BECAUSE I HAVE GREAT FAITH IN YOU. ALSO BECAUSE I HAVE A LOT OF BETS ON YOU!'

May 29, 1981

'QUICK! ONE RUBBER DUCKIE, ONE PACIFIER, MORE SAFETY PINS, MORE TALCUM POWDER, MORE PLASTIC PANTS AND MORE DIAPERS — I GOTTA GET BACK TO THE LITTLE PESTS!'

June 1, 1981

THE STOCKMAN RICKSHAW: wherewith the Elderly find fulfilling employment in their Golden Years, and a national mass-transit crisis is Averted.
WHENCE?
OLIPHANT

June 2, 1981

O'NEILL, WRIGHT, AND OTHER LEADING DEMOCRATS, LEAVE THE WHITE HOUSE AFTER HAVING CONVINCED THE PRESIDENT THEY MEAN BUSINESS ON THE TAX CUTS.

June 3, 1981

'THANKYOU, CONGRESSMAN, FOR THIS TRULY WONDERFUL NEW WEAP...'

June 4, 1981

'I'LL HAVE TO ASK YOU TO LOWER YOUR EXPECTATIONS A LITTLE.'

June 5, 1981

THE CORNUCOPIA OF THE BLESSED SAINT WATT

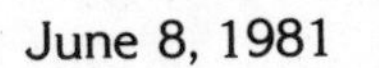

June 8, 1981

LITTLE LADY, ALL I CAN SAY IS, IF SOMEBODY RAPED ME AND I GOT PREGNANT, I CERTAINLY WOULDN'T HAVE AN ABORTION!
HELMS
JESSE, IN YOUR CASE YOU COULD MAKE AN EXCEPTION

June 9, 1981

'LET'S SEE IF I'VE GOT THIS DEAL STRAIGHT, MR. PRESIDENT . . . FOR EVERY BARREL OF MEXICAN OIL WE BUY, WE GET ONE FREE BARREL OF MEXICAN NATIONALS?'

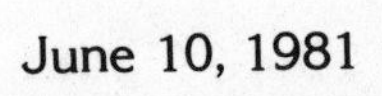
June 10, 1981

VOTE FOR THE SELF-DEFENSE PEACE CANDIDATE
HELLUVA WAY TO CAMPAIGN!
OLIPHANT

June 11, 1981

SOVIET CONTROL
POLISH INDEPENDENCE
EITHER WAY YOU GET DEVOURED
OLIPHANT

June 12, 1981

F-16 MADE IN U.S.A.
DEFENSIVE USE ONLY!
ANY OFFENSIVE USE OF THIS
AIRCRAFT WILL RESULT IN
A WRIST-SLAPPING
OLIPHANT

June 15, 1981

'OH, NO, SIR, IT'S NOT FOR A TEAM OWNER. IT'S FOR MY OWNER — HE'S A PLAYER!'

June 16, 1981

I'M AT MY WITS' END DOCTOR—
THIS KID IS 33 YEARS OLD, BUT HE GOES AROUND THE HOUSE SMASHING THINGS UP, SETTING FIRE TO THE DRAPES...
HAVE YOU TRIED SAYING 'NO' TO THE SPOILED LITTLE TWERP?
CHILD PSYCHIATRIST
U.N. APPROVED
WATCH IT, DOC— HE'LL BURN YOUR OFFICE DOWN!
OLIPHANT

June 17, 1981

'OH, WELL — UNDER THE CIRCUMSTANCES, I DON'T SUPPOSE THEY'LL TOO MUCH MIND BEING TWO TO A CELL.'

June 18, 1981

ASK HIM, 'WHAT ABOUT TAIWAN?'
HE SAYS, 'WHAT ABOUT TAIWAN?'
TELL HIM THOSE ARE OUR SENTIMENTS EXACTLY
OLIPHANT

June 19, 1981

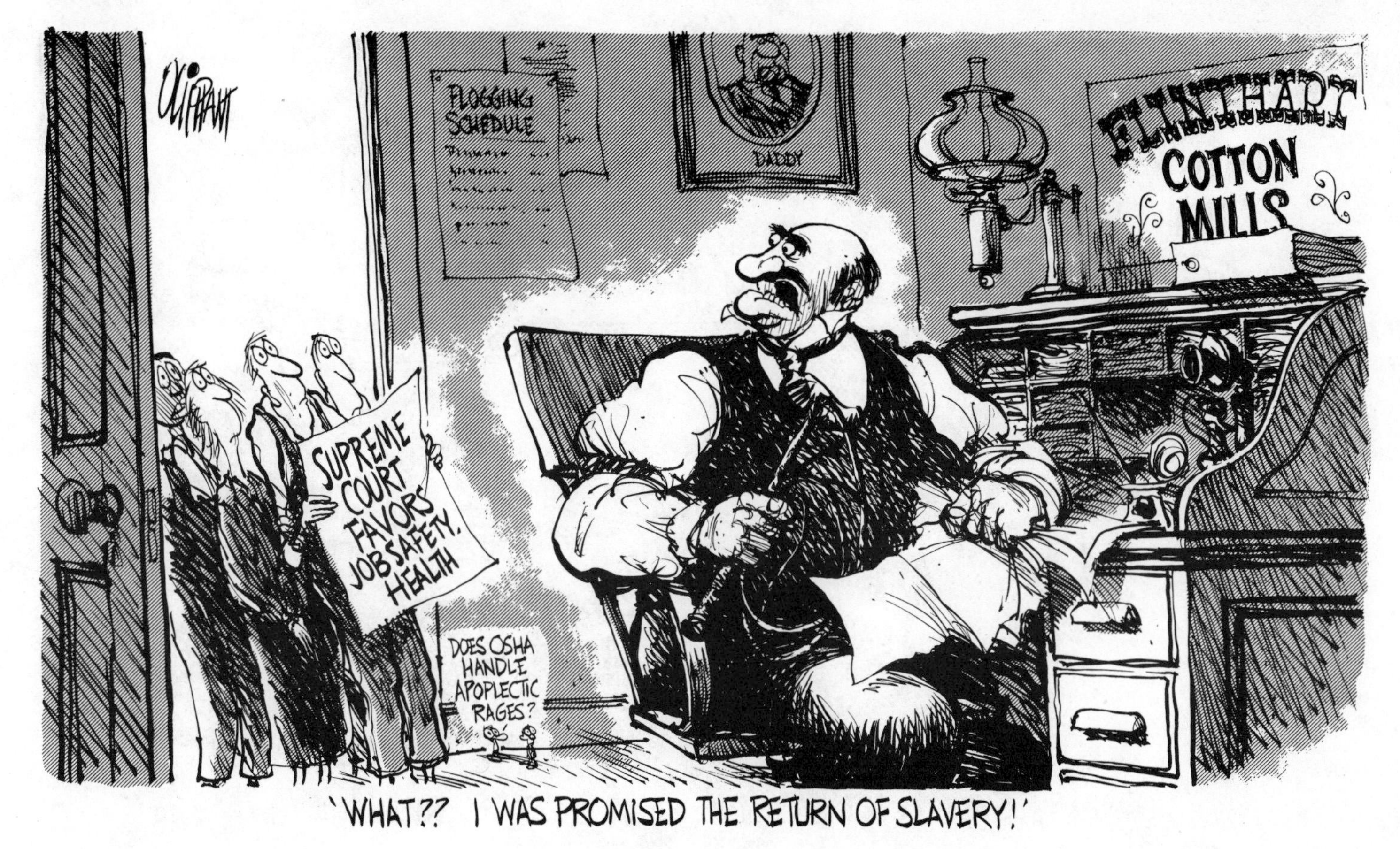

'WHAT?? I WAS PROMISED THE RETURN OF SLAVERY!'

June 22, 1981

'THE GIRLS CONGRATULATE YOU ON THIS GREAT OPPORTUNITY.'

June 23, 1981

'AIR TRAFFIC CONTROL TO CAPTAIN REAGAN — YOU TAKE CARE, NOW.'

June 24, 1981

'UNDER THE NEW STANDARDS FOR AIR PURITY, WE WILL IN FUTURE APPLY THE WATT-GORSUCH TEST. IF YOU CAN'T FEEL ANY LUMPS IN IT, IT'S OK.'

June 25, 1981

'THERE, THERE, MASTER McENROE...'

June 26, 1981

...ANYONE KNOWING OF ANY REASON WHY FRANCOIS MITTERRAND SHOULD NOT MARRY THIS...
OLIPHANT
COMMUNISTS
BUSH
MARRIAGE IS A SOVEREIGN STATE, GEORGE

June 29, 1981

'NEXT TIME HE TELLS YOU HE LIVED SO CLOSE TO THE WRONG SIDE OF THE TRACKS HE COULD HEAR THE WHISTLE, WELL, YOU CAN JUST SAY TO HIM, "OH, YEAH?".'

June 30, 1981

'WE, THE POOR, FEEL YOU SHOULD HAUL YOURSELF UP BY YOUR OWN BOOTSTRAPS.'

July 1, 1981

THE PASSING OF FRED SILVERMAN

July 2, 1981

July 6, 1981

THE NEW COLORS

July 7, 1981

'AH, YES, WHIPSNADE, MY BOY — MY RETIREMENT-AGE CREDITORS ARE BECOMING A TRIFLE UGLY. MAY I TROUBLE YOU FOR A SMALL DEBT-CONSOLIDATION LOAN..?'

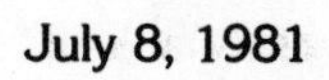
July 8, 1981

AND THE SUPREME COURT NOMINEE IS
YOU SAY HE'S RUINING AMERICA?
FOR US DEMOCRATS HE IS!

July 9, 1981

OLIPHANT
THE JERRY FALWELL CHURCH OF THE MORAL PEJORATIVE — A TAX-FREE ORGANIZATION
WOULD THAT BE IN THE KITCHEN, SIR? OR, BAREFOOT AND PREGNANT, PERHAPS?
'SUPREME COURT, INDEED! GET BACK IN YOUR PLACE, WOMAN!'

July 10, 1981

OLIPHANT
COURAGE, GWENDOLYN—NOBODY WITH ANY MANNERS WILL NOTICE!
U.K. MAYHEM (Ahem!)
ROYAL WEDDING INVITATION
CARRY ON

July 13, 1981

HEY, LIKE, I'M SORRY, MAN
LIKE, I DIG FLIES AND
OTHER BIRDS, Y'KNOW...
BUT REAGAN SAYS THIS
IS A JOB FOR
CAPTAIN
MALATHION,
MAN...
BROWN
CHOMP
PHONE
WHAT'S
HE BEEN
SNIFFIN'
NOW?
OLIPHANT